The Deltora Book of Monsters

by Josef

Palace Librarian in the reign of King Alton

Text by Emily Rodda

Illustrations by Marc McBride

SCHOLASTIC INC.

New York   Toronto   London   Auckland   Sydney   Mexico City   New Delhi   Hong Kong   Buenos Aires

ISBN 0-439-39084-2

First published in 2001. Text copyright © Emily Rodda.
Deltora Quest concept and characters copyright © Emily Rodda.
Illustrations copyright © Scholastic Australia, 2000.
Illustrations by Marc McBride.

All rights reserved. Published by Scholastic Inc., 557 Broadway, New York, NY 10012 by arrangement with Scholastic Press, an imprint of Scholastic Australia.

SCHOLASTIC and associated logos are trademarks and/or registered trademarks of Scholastic, Inc.

12 11 10 9 8 7 6 5 4 3 2 1   2 3 4 5 6 7/0

Printed in the U.S.A.   23

First Scholastic printing, June 2002

Foreword

This book has been compiled in secret. If the work had been discovered by any in authority, I, its author, would have paid with my life. Or so I believe.

The risk was worth taking. Forces are working in Deltora to suppress the facts of our past as well as those of our present. Lies are everywhere. King Alton believes that the kingdom is thriving. He thinks that if monstrous perils once existed in far-flung corners, they exist no longer.

I know this is false. Because I, who once wore the silken gloves and velvet tunic of a palace librarian, now scavenge for food in the gutters of Del. I now know what the common people know, and more. I could never have imagined such a future for myself. But I regret nothing.

Perhaps I would never have fled from the palace if the king's chief advisor, Prandine, had not ordered me to burn *The Deltora Annals*. It grieves me to think that future readers of this book ⌈if any there be⌉ may never have heard of the *Annals*. But it could be so, and therefore I must explain it as best I can.

The *Annals*, a day-to-day "journal" of Deltoran tales and news, was begun shortly after the seven tribes of this land joined under the leadership of the great Adin, drove the Shadow Lord's hordes back across the mountains, and formed a united Deltora. Its many volumes, now safely hidden where I hope no enemy can find them, record Deltora's oldest times. The first volume includes all the stories, legends, and histories of the seven tribes. Some of these ⌈such as the Jalis tribe's "Tenna Birdsong Tales" — stories supposedly told to a young girl called Tenna by a blackbird she had released from a net⌉ had never before appeared in written form.

Work on the *Annals* continued for centuries, but was abandoned in the time of Queen Elspeth, the present king's great-grandmother. Elspeth's chief advisor said that the palace writers and painters should devote themselves to the far more important task of describing and drawing the palace, room by room. Queen Elspeth let him have his way. As, I fear, King Alton bows to Prandine's will today.

Once work on the *Annals* ceased, the writers and painters were no longer permitted to leave the palace, for their work was all within. The palace's last contact with the outside world was lost. I have often wondered if this was the chief advisor's real aim, all the time.

When he told me to destroy the *Annals*, Prandine claimed that the king had commanded it, because the old volumes were riddled with errors and took up valuable space. In fact, they had long been kept in a library storeroom, so neither King Alton nor his son, Prince Endon, had ever seen them. Prandine said there would be a new history of Deltora — a thing of beauty, containing no "foolish" folk stories, no "fanciful" travellers' tales, or "incorrect" ideas.

I knew what that meant. It meant grand appearance, grand statements, and little else. It meant our past according to Prandine. By all means, write a new history, I thought. But why destroy the old? Unless you fear it, because it contains things you want forgotten. The threatened destruction of the *Annals*, that great, vivid picture of Deltora over the ages, was more than I could bear. Besides, I had spent my life caring for books, and did not care to begin burning them. And so it was that while pretending to obey Prandine's order ⌈for I knew well the dangers of open rebellion⌉ I saved the *Annals* and myself.

To this day, I hope, Prandine believes I perished in the fire I lit in the storeroom. The note I left, stating that I wanted to die with the *Annals* was, I hope, convincing. The bones found in the wreckage would have helped. I have read that animal and human bones look very alike when fire has crumbled them to dust. I hope also that Prandine still thinks that the mass of ash found in that room was all that remained of **The Deltora Annals**. I regretted burning the old harvest records, but I had no choice. The **Annals** and I left the palace at the bottom of a rubbish cart. I did not like treating them, or myself, in so undignified a fashion, but it was the only possible means of escape. My only thought was to save the **Annals**. I had no idea of the suffering I would find outside the palace gates. I did not know how foolish had been my belief that, working in the comfort of my library, I understood how things were in Deltora. I was to learn much, in the days to come.

This book uses material drawn from **The Deltora Annals** as well as new information I have gained in the past few years. It describes many of the dreadful, mysterious beings that haunt this land. The pictures are as accurate as I can make them, but occasionally I have had to use my imagination — readers must forgive any small errors I may have made as a result.

Some of these creatures are as evil and unnatural as their master in the Shadowlands. Others are native to Deltora. All grow stronger every day. Yet the king does nothing to offer his people protection. They hate him for it. But why should he help, since he does not know the monsters exist? None of them are spoken of in the palace except as beasts of legend, dangers of the past.

Books such as this are needed to correct the lies that have become official truth. The people are too busy scraping a living to write down what they know. Writing, in fact, seems almost to have disappeared among them. I fear that lies may one day be the only "facts" available to students, unless people like me act to prevent it.

Now that the book is finished, I wonder what will become of it. Do I dare hope that one day, in less dangerous times, it will be found and used by Deltoran students and travellers? Or even copied widely, to be read by people from other lands? Perhaps. For now it is enough for me to know that it is done.

My work is not ended, however. At last I have a safe workplace — the cellar of Deltora's largest pottery. I was introduced to its kind owners by a pedlar called Steven, who once saved my life. Steven suggested that when I had finished this book, I might begin a new volume of **The Deltora Annals**. And so I will, with the help of my young apprentice, Ranesh, who collects news as cleverly as he once picked pockets. What the future holds for us, and for Deltora, I cannot say. But when my hopes dim, I take heart by remembering another thing I did before I left the palace. It concerns yet another book — far smaller and older than this one. Its name is **The Belt of Deltora**. It is simply written, but full of wisdom. From the day I first found it in the library, I believed that it was of vital importance, and that it contained the keys to Deltora's future, as well as its past. I kept it hidden, for I knew that if Prandine saw it, it would quietly disappear. I had planned to take it with me, but at the last moment something moved me to change my mind. I hid it, instead, in a dim corner where it would only be discovered by an eager searcher.

I cling to the hope that one day Prince Endon might find it. Even Endon's friend, young Jarred, might do so, for though Jarred has no great love of books, his wits are keen. He may remember the library if one day he is in urgent need of knowledge. I know in my heart that if Deltora has a future, it lies with these young ones. It would be my joy to know that in some small way I have helped their cause. In faith —

Josef
Writing in the city of Del in the 35th year of the reign of King Alton.

Contents

Soldeen

oldeen is the first monster in this book, for he was the reason I began it. He haunts my dreams, and I fear he always will. Soldeen lurks in the murky depths of the Lake of Tears. Normally he feeds on the blind, crawling things that infest his hideous domain, but he will ravenously attack anyone or anything foolish enough to set foot on his shore.

Created by the sorcery of Thaegan [see The Sorceress Thaegan, p. 12], Soldeen can breathe both air and water, and is able to speak. He can swim with great speed, and will throw himself onto the lake's shore in pursuit of food.

I learned of Soldeen on the night of my escape from the palace. I had found shelter in a small inn, telling the surly innkeeper I was a traveller. He did not believe me, and no wonder. My clothes, and the books I carried, made my story unlikely. He took the ring I offered, however, and gave me a dirty attic where clearly no one had stayed for years. He guessed I would not complain.

His meanness was a stroke of luck. Looking for a place to store my books, I found, in a dusty cupboard, a jumbled heap of things left by previous tenants. Among them were pages of Ralad writing, and drawings of a gigantic beast. The drawings were labelled SOLDEEN. The writings [which fortunately I could understand, having learned Ralad script as a child] told of a monster who guarded the Lake of Tears, killing all who ventured into his domain.

Possibly the Ralad travellers who once stayed in that attic had meant to take the papers to the palace. Some misfortune had plainly overtaken them before they could complete their mission. The mission was doomed anyway. If the papers had been delivered, they would surely have been destroyed before the king saw them. As it was, they were thrown into a cupboard by a lazy innkeeper and at last found by me.

My candle burned low as I read of the terror of Soldeen and the sufferings of Raladin. I shuddered as I studied the images that the Ralad artists had made. I saw that evils beyond anything I had ever imagined were abroad in Deltora. By the time dawn broke, I knew that I had more to do than guard Deltora's memories. I had to use what talents I possessed to record the evils of its present as well. And thus the idea for this book was born.

Gorl

A fearsome being clad in the armor of a Jalis knight, Gorl is said to guard the dark center of Mid Wood, the smallest of the three Forests of Silence. Legend has it that Gorl possesses supernatural strength and has the power to bend others to his will. Suspicious and jealous of his territory, he challenges all intruders, killing without mercy if his warning to flee is ignored. This story of a terrifying knight-presence haunting Mid Wood is an ancient one, having been told since before the joining of the seven tribes. **The Deltora Annals** contain more than fifty references to Gorl.

These are based only on the tales of travellers. Possibly they are simply reports of nightmarish visions produced by the terror of the Forests. It is interesting to note, however, that in all the accounts the details of the knight do not vary. In addition, the sketches made by those who have claimed to have seen Gorl and escaped with their lives, while varying widely in artistic skill, bear remarkable similarities to one another.

The origin of the Gorl legend, if legend it be, can probably be traced to a Jalis folktale that is even older than the Gorl story itself. It is called "The Tale of the Three Knights," and is one of the "Tenna Birdsong" stories. It concerns three brothers, Jalis knights, who travelled to the Forests of Silence to seek the fabled Lilies of Life. The brothers at last found their prize only to begin fighting over it until the two youngest had perished at the hands of their older brother. The names of the slain knights were Greddock and Gudden. Their murdering brother was — Gorl.

Gorl is a common name among the Jalis. But since in the tale the brothers find the Lilies of Life in "the Forests' dark center," we may surely guess at a link with the Gorl legend. Whether the link is one of fancy or of truth, who can say? But if it is truth, as this writer suspects, then the magic that has kept the being called Gorl alive and menacing over such ages is dark and powerful indeed.

The Wennbar and the Wenn

The Wennbar is a gross beast whose territory is First Wood – the Forest of Silence which is most near to Del.

Its slaves are the Wenn, a strange tribe of cold-blooded beings over which it seems to exert complete control.

The Wenn, which themselves eat only the leaves of certain bushes, trap humans and animals that stray into their path so as to provide the Wennbar with the warm flesh it prefers for food. By rubbing their lower legs together they make a high-pitched ringing sound unbearable to the ears of more advanced creatures. They then sting and paralyze their disabled prey and offer it to the Wennbar as a helpless, living sacrifice.

This partnership between Wenn and Wennbar is mysterious, and does not seem to be an equal one. According to *The Deltora Annals*, the Wenn worship the Wennbar as a god. The monster's pleasure at receiving food is their only reward. Its anger when cheated of prey usually means the death of one or more of them. Yet they do not rebel, but glory in their slavery.

Generally slow and heavy in its movements, the Wennbar is said to move extremely quickly when hungry or filled with anger. In addition, its neck, usually hidden in folds of flesh, can rapidly extend to enormous lengths, so that it can snatch creatures from trees and birds from the air.

By all accounts, there has only ever been one Wennbar, and the Wenn have always lived in the bushy grove called Wen Del that guards the entrance to its territory. Legend has it that every hundred years the Wennbar goes into a deep sleep and, having been bathed in special oils by the Wenn, dies giving birth to several young.

The young fight each other to the death over the motionless body of their parent. The victor is the new Wennbar, destined to be tyrant over the Wenn for the next century.

The Sorceress Thaegan

The rise of a powerful sorceress in Deltora's northeast was first noted in **The Deltora Annals** during the last years of Queen Elspeth the present king's great-grandmother.

The Sorceress Thaegan is said to have inherited her magical abilities from her mother, a wisewoman named Tamm. Tamm was much respected by her neighbors in the northern village of Nest, for she could make successful love potions and cast healing spells. It was also said that she could transform herself into a blackbird at will.

Thaegan's powers were much stronger than Tamm's, however, and, unhappily, though the girl was beautiful to look upon, her nature was cruel and spiteful. Bored by her mother's simple life, she turned to dark magic to satisfy her taste for power. Tamm tried to reason with her, and finally to control her, but to no avail. Thaegan broke through the shutting spell Tamm had woven around their cottage, and fled into the mountains that separate Deltora from the Shadowlands.

We cannot know what happened to her there, or what hideous bargain she may have struck with the evil forces she summoned to her hideaway. We only know that when she came down from the mountains again, seven years later, she was more powerful than any sorceress Deltora had ever seen, and her reign of terror over the north began.

Nearly a hundred years have passed, but the Sorceress Thaegan is today still alive and more powerful than ever. Her malice has increased with age. She is said to relish blackbirds for food — no doubt in spiteful memory of her mother. Despite a life of wickedness that has spanned over a century, she continues to have the appearance of a beautiful woman. The dread horror that must lurk beneath this illusion can only be imagined.

Witches, it is said, can be killed by drawing blood, but Thaegan is free from the fear of injury, for she is armored by magic. Her body shines green as glass — protected by a surface that no arrow or spear can injure. The only exception is the tip of one little finger, the finger with which she casts her vile spells.

Though the king continues to be unaware of her existence, the people know of her only too well. Few now dare to travel through her territory. Those who have done so in the past have either never returned, or crawled back to their homes stricken in body and mind. Vast areas of countryside in the north have been laid waste. Notable among these wastelands is the hideous Lake of Tears [see Soldeen, p. 6], which floods the place where once shone the golden towers of D'Or.

Thaegan destroyed D'Or out of pure hatred — hatred of its beauty and its people's happiness. When the neighboring folk of Raladin cried out against the destruction, she took away their voices so they could speak no more.

The Sorceress Thaegan has thirteen children, all of them foul, monstrous beings which aid her in her tyranny and plunder the countryside. They are not as powerful as their mother but like her can create illusions and transform their shapes at will. Whether they were fathered by the forces of darkness or simply brought forth by Thaegan on her own account is not known.

Thaegan's Children

he names of Thaegan's evil brood are: Hot, Tot, Pik, Snik, Jin, Jod, Fie, Fly, Zan, Zod, Lun, Lod, and Ichabod. I gained knowledge of their names and appearance from an unfortunate man I found cringing by the city gates. He was ragged and starving. His mind had been clouded by horror. He was the only one of five travellers to have escaped the clutches of Thaegan's children. His companions were roasted alive and eaten. He was to be the last in the fire, but before his time came the monsters, bloated, fell asleep. He managed to escape to stumble back to Del.

He could not even remember his own name, but the picture of Thaegan's children as he had seen them was burned into his brain. From his hideous descriptions this picture was painted.

Jin is green-white, and grossly fat. She has yellow tusks, and three stubby horns sprout from the back of her skull. Jod has metal spikes for teeth, and there are just two flaring nostrils where his nose should be. Fie and Fly are green with large heads and dripping brown fangs. Hot and Tot are small and yellow. Zan has six stumpy legs. Pik and Snik are covered in brown hair. Lan and Lod are pale and bald. Zod is covered in lumps. Ichabod is huge, and slimy red. I have not labelled the monsters. But you, dear reader, can I am sure pick out which one is which. Unless you wish simply to turn your gaze away, and flick over the page. I would not blame you.

Grey Guards

rey Guards, slavish servants of the Shadow Lord, appear human, but are monsters in the truest sense. Created by their master to enforce his evil will, they lack all normal human emotions, relishing cruelty and destruction above all else. They have great physical strength, are capable of enormous speed and endurance, have keen sight and hearing, and frequently hunt by scent. Their chief weapons are leather slings with which they hurl egg-shaped missiles known as "blisters." Blisters burst on contact, releasing a burning poison that causes agonizing death. Grey Guards have no understanding of the terms "mother" and "father," and live, work, and fight in clan groups, or "pods," of ten. Each member of a single pod is identical with his brothers [female Guards are unknown]. Most observers believe that pod members are "born" together, probably as mature adults, by some vile means as yet not understood. All Guards are known by their pod name followed by a number. Members of the Carn pod [pictured], for example, will be called Carn 1, Carn 2, and so on till Carn 10 is reached.

In ancient days Grey Guards, then rarely seen in Deltora, were thought to be immortal. It is now known that, though they do not age visibly, they suddenly weaken and die after seven years. The mistaken belief in their immortality arose because when the members of any one pod near their "fail date" [as the seven-year limit is known], they are recalled to the Shadowlands and replaced by a fresh set of ten bearing the same pod name, and with exactly the same appearance.

The Seven Ak-Baba

These ferocious creatures first appeared in Deltoran skies in the last years before the rise of Adin. They were identified as Ak-Baba – huge, vulturelike birds said to live a thousand years, and previously seen only by travellers to distant lands. *The Deltora Annals* contain several descriptions of Ak-Baba from the days when Deltoran sea trade and exploration were common [days sadly long gone].

It is now recognized, however, that the seven Ak-Baba patrolling Deltora are wild birds. They are creatures of the Shadow Lord, used to spy, destroy, and accomplish tasks that require great speed. They are more ferocious than their wild cousins, and, as well as feeding on dead flesh, will attack living creatures without hesitation. They possess teeth as well as a tearing beak and claws. A foul smell surrounds them, lingering for hours after they have departed. And, most important, their minds appear to be linked to that of the Shadow Lord, for they do his will without spoken command. Our conclusion must be that they have been altered, or bred, to suit the Shadow Lord's purposes.

No weapon has yet proved successful against them. Even the mighty winged Dragons of old could not defeat them. Several eyewitness reports of terrible sky battles between single Dragons and up to five of the Seven Ak-Baba are included in **The Deltora Annals.** The fights raged for days, but always the Dragon was at last destroyed. It is no doubt the Seven Ak-Baba are responsible for the gradual decline in Deltoran Dragon numbers, and their present [believed] extinction [see Dragons, p. 46].

Reeah

One of Deltora's greatest mysteries is the fabled City of the Rats. An old, walled city on a barren plain, it is without human life. Its people abandoned it long ago, fleeing from the rats which infested their halls. Details in the **Annals** are few, for the city [then called Hira] was isolated. It lay in a bend of the River Broad, and could only be reached from the north.

The first report, in the time of King Brandon, tells of the beginning of the Hira rat plague. The last, fifty years later, is by a wanderer called Rue, who helped dig a canal to separate "the Plain of the Rats" from an orchard to its north. He enjoyed this [despite the "fierce bees" swarming in the orchard] for he received in return: "food, shelter, and excellent Cider twice a day."

Before leaving, Rue crossed the canal and visited the deserted city on the plain. He dared not enter, for "it seethed with vicious rats, fighting for space and breath, the living feasting upon the dead."

Some say Hira's rat plague was a curse. But I believe it was part of a sinister plan, for I know the city's evil secret. The rats are only food for a far greater terror. A young pedlar called Steven told me this. He said he and his brother had decided I should know. When asked how they knew of it, and of me, he said: "The bees told us." He sounds mad, perhaps. Yet I know he told me the truth.

Deep within the City of the Rats there is a giant snake called Reeah. Its body is as thick as an ancient tree trunk, and vast enough to fill a great hall. Its vanity and wickedness know no bounds.

How did it come to the city? Who is the one it calls its Master? Why do Ak-Baba so often hover above its lair in Deltora's heart?

I fear I know the answers to these questions.

They fill me with dread.

the nine Ra-Kacharz

The ruthless beings known as the Nine Ra-Kacharz are not mentioned in **The Deltora Annals**. There is no marketplace chatter concerning them. Yet the Nine exist, there is no doubt. As soon as I heard rumor of them, I began to hunt for details. So great is the fear they inspire that those who have seen them are reluctant to speak. The facts I have gathered are these:

The Ra-Kacharz rule in the closed city of Noradz, a grim place where visitors are unwelcome and life is constant toil. Noradz is within the area of the Plains, but travellers should not venture near it, or try to penetrate its secrets. Others who have done so have disappeared, or only narrowly escaped with their lives.

This is because Noradz is a city of strange beliefs and rituals, an of rigid rules. The penalty for disobedience is often death, and ignoranc of the law is no excuse. The Ra-Kacharz are the priests wh enforce the rules.

Their close-fitting scarlet clothing is the mark of their office. Their eyes, the only parts of their bodies to be visible, are cold as the stones of the city walls. Their people regard them with terrified awe. They are rumored to be immortal. They carry long plaited leather whips, which they use freely to threaten and to punish.

They are the only citizens of Noradz who may leave the city, and they always travel in pairs. They are usually seen driving loaded carts, or riding odd, unruly beasts called Muddlets [see Muddlets, p. 24]. If they meet strangers on the road they do not even look at them, but pass by staring straight ahead.

By all accounts, this is just as well. Travellers are advised not to attempt to attract their attention. To be noticed by a Ra-Kachar of Noradz is highly dangerous.

23

Muddlets

Perhaps some will consider that I am wrong to include Muddlets in this book. Muddlets are not "monsters" in the sense of being savage or wicked. They do not have teeth, claws, spines, or poison. They eat only grass, moss, apples, and certain leaves. And they are by all reports very good-natured.

Nevertheless, they are such strange, self-willed creatures that I decided they deserved a place in this collection. They have carried many unknowing riders into danger.

Wild herds of Muddlets once roamed the Plains country, especially in the area now known as the Plain of the Rats [see Reeah, p. 20]. According to *The Deltora Annals* they numbered many, many thousands, and to be caught in a Muddlet stampede was a terrifying and life-threatening experience. Over the years, as towns and villages grew and the Plain of the Rats was eaten bare by the multiplying rats, herd numbers grew less. Wild Muddlets are now rarely seen, though they still exist.

Muddlets have extraordinary speed and strength. For thousands of years they have been captured by Plains people for use as beasts of burden. But they do not make reliable domestic animals.

However tame they may seem, they cannot be relied upon to do anything other than what they wish. No matter what their training may have been, for example, they will bolt at the sight of any small, furred animal. They will also ignore all instructions if they smell their home field or over-ripe apples [their favorite food], even plunging into deep water, over cliffs, and into quicksand to reach their goal.

Despite this, Muddlets are still used by some Plains folk. The Ra-Kacharz of Noradz [see The Nine Ra-Kacharz p. 22] are among those who still keep a Muddlet herd. But any traveller who may be tempted by the Muddlets' low price should think twice before following their example. Muddlets are not beasts to trust.

25

Sand Beasts

These ferocious creatures prowl the Shifting Sands, a place of barren dunes which lies within the homeland of the Mere tribe. They are properly called Terreocti, but are better known as Sand Beasts. Long before the united Deltora was formed, the Shifting Sands had become forbidden territory. Our only information about Sand Beasts, therefore, comes from Mere records of the distant past.

Sand Beasts are ferocious hunters. They are skilled at catching the lizards which abound in their territory, but prefer larger prey. Their usual method is to burrow through the dunes towards an unsuspecting victim, then leap out and attack with terrifying speed.

The Deltora Annals records that in ancient days the Mere would force the worst of their criminals to walk into the Sands. The same fate awaited Plains prisoners taken during the battles over territory which often occurred between the tribes. Sand Beasts would attack the doomed persons within minutes.

It was a particularly cruel and savage form of execution which Mere folk of more modern times would, naturally enough, prefer not to discuss. Almost all the known facts on Sand Beast behavior were collected by a woman known as Rigane the Mad. Rigane lived in a hut beside the Shifting Sands for over forty years. She was fascinated by the place and its creatures, and left many notes and sketches describing them. Rigane's notes, reproduced in The Deltora Annals, tell us that Sand Beasts are perfectly adapted to the harsh conditions of their desert home. Prey provides them with both food and drink. The hard "shell" that covers their bodies protects them from the sun, and from the rasping effects of the sand.

Perhaps their most amazing feature is their way of raising their young. Between four and sixteen leathery "stomachs" hang outside their bodies, like grapes on a stem. The older the creature is, the more stomachs it possesses.

When one of these stomachs is completely filled, it tears away from the Beast's body and falls onto the sand. If the Beast is female, the stomach is then pierced and an egg is laid inside it. A male Beast must drum his feet on the sand until a female answers his call and lays an egg for him.

Many find this system repulsive, but I agree with Rigane that it is clever. The leathery skin of the stomach protects the egg from both sun and

the lizards. The hatchling can feed on the stomach's contents until it is big enough to break free and begin hunting for itself.

I well understand Rigane's fascination with Sand Beasts, though I would not have cared to examine them as closely as she did. Some of her observations were made from the roof of her hut, but most resulted from the journeys she made into the Sands.

On these expeditions she wore a sand-colored, hooded cloak and boots of her own invention. The boots' soles were as big as snow-sleds and made of closely woven cane. Rigane claimed that they allowed her to slide over the dunes without creating too much vibration. She believed that the Sand Beasts had little sense of hearing, but rather felt the approach of prey.

Possibly she was right, for she survived no less than five treks into the Sands. On her return from the last of these, she claimed to have reached the center and there to have found an extraordinary structure she called "The Hive".

Most people believed that this story was fantasy, and proof of Rigane's madness. I am not sure what to think.

Her insistence that she was "drawn," to the center seems indeed a sign of madness. The way she calls strange markings in the sand "messages" is also odd. As is her comment that the sand becomes "angry" when disturbed, creating whirlwinds and weird shapes to terrify intruders. It is as if she believes the sand is a living thing.

Her other notes, however, are as clear as always. And I have learned that many strange things exist in our land—things that once I would never have believed. For this reason I have included a painting of "The Hive" on the following pages, using Rigane's sketches as models. Readers must decide for themselves whether it was something Rigane actually saw, or merely imagined.

After the fifth journey, Rigane stayed in her hut, working on her notes, for many months.

The Hive

When she emerged, she began engraving words on a large stone. These warned strangers of the Shifting Sands, and included a mysterious rhyme.

Rigane had the engraved stone taken to the nearest road, and placed where passers-by could see it. I hear it is still there, though the engraving is now so worn that the words of the rhyme are almost lost. I would dearly love to see it for myself.

Soon after placing the stone, Rigane made her sixth journey into the Shifting Sands. She never returned, and it was thought that she had at last fallen victim to a Sand Beast.

But I wonder. The letter she left behind with the notes and drawings that represented her life's work, read simply: "I must return to the Center. I can no longer resist the call, though I know it will mean my death. My bones will serve the Hive. I am content.
Rigane."

The Mere tribe eventually closed in the Sands, piling huge boulders into heaps to make a thick, high wall. Folklore holds that this was done to stop the spread — the "growth," it was called — of the Shifting Sands. The Sands, it is said, were creeping outward.

Most educated people dismiss this story, though it cannot be denied that the Sands were, indeed, slowly increasing in area. **The Deltora Annals** note that by the time the wall was complete, sand had completely covered Rigane's hut and the surrounding area.

I must agree, however, that it is far more likely that the wall was built to cage the Sand Beasts. These had been growing in number, due, no doubt, to the appalling practice of casting prisoners into the Sands. All species multiply more rapidly when nourishing food is plentiful. The labor on the wall was long. Thousands of Mere workers spent whole lifetimes on the task, and many of the best-known Mere folk songs [the most famous of which is the rollicking ballad "Walling the Sands"] tell of the tragedies, loves, and exciting events that occurred during those years.

In the time of Adin, land was cleared outside the wall, and a fence was built between the resulting plain and the road. After that, the Shifting Sands was left severely alone. No doubt the Sand Beast population dropped as a result. Lizards are not very rich fare.

And as for the sand itself — who can tell? But sometimes I think of Rigane's last words, and, looking at my own painting, wonder where her bones lie. And whether, as she predicted, she serves The Hive, even after death.

Gellick

The giant toad Gellick rules in Dread Mountain. The idea is shocking to anyone who knows Deltoran history, but it is true.

The Mountain in Deltora's northwest corner has always been the domain of the Dread Gnomes. Tales of their courage and fighting skill stud the pages of **The Deltora Annals** like gems from their own treasure hoard. But Dread Mountain is very near the Shadowlands border. For years the Gnomes have had to battle wave after wave of the Shadow Lord's Guards [see Grey Guards, p. 16] and fighting beasts [see Vraal, p. 36] sent to enslave them.

Now the toad Gellick, crawling from its lair deep in the rocks further north, has persuaded the Gnomes to serve it in return for a powerful weapon. Poisonous slime oozes from its skin—a venom so strong that a single drop is deadly. With this on their arrows, the Gnomes can defeat any invader.

I fear they have paid a terrible price. The toad speaks soft words for now, perhaps, but it is hiding its true nature. The **Annals** call it a vile beast, greedy, cruel and swollen with conceit. I heard of the Gnomes' plight this way:

I had sold a gold chain — my last valuable possession — to buy paper, paint, and food. I was sitting in the market, eating ravenously, for I was starving. A small brown hand seized my wrist. Startled, I looked up at a figure in a hooded cloak. It was a Dread Gnome, the first I had ever seen. "I can trust you," she said. "You eat, and you are warm." Naturally, I thought she was mad. I was to learn otherwise.

Her name was Sha-Ban. She had fled from Dread Mountain planning to beg the king's help for her people. But after a single day in Del she knew her quest was hopeless. The king was shut away, out of her reach. As he was out of the reach of all of us.

When she had told me of Gellick she began to speak of her journey, and the terrible things she had seen. I thought she had drifted into a nightmarish fantasy, and hoped the two old fruit-sellers near us would not hear her and be terrified. Fool that I was! Sha-Ban was doomed. It did not suit the Enemy to have her news spread in Del. I went to buy more bread. When I returned, she was lying, strangled and icy cold, in a pile of rotten fruit. The fruit-sellers had vanished.

I confess with shame that I left the brave Gnome where she lay, and ran. I knew I was a hunted man, for what Sha-Ban knew, I now knew also. But I vowed that the news she had given her life to tell would not die with her.

Ols

When first I heard of Ols, I did not believe in them. I nearly paid for that mistake with my life.

The Dread Gnome Sha-Ban told me of these white, formless creatures that could take the shape of any living thing — human, animal, or even insect. When attacking, she said, Ols emerge from their disguise, rising like ghastly, flickering white flames with holes for eyes, gaping, toothless mouths, and strangling hands. She said that Ols had been created by the Shadow Lord and sent into Deltora in the hundreds to spy and kill. She insisted that in the countryside everyone knew of Ols, and feared them. In my conceit, I doubted her. Surely, I reasoned, if Ols were so well known I would have heard of them. I forgot that Sha-Ban was the first traveller in years to bring fresh news from the west. I soothed her as if she were a child with nightmares, saying there were no Ols in Del. I did not consider that Ols might be all about me — listening, watching, spreading lies — doing their master's evil work in secret. I bitterly regret my foolishness. Everything Sha-Ban told me was true, and she paid for the telling with her life.

After I found her dead I ran to the inn, collected my things, and crept out the back way. Through a window I saw the two fruit-sellers from the market talking to the innkeeper. He pointed towards the attic. They nodded, and strolled to the stairs. I looked at them carefully and saw they were Ols, and the killers of Sha-Ban. I knew I would be their next victim if they could find me. I left hastily.

You too, dear reader, must learn the signs by which Ols can be recognized. One day your life may depend upon it. To help you, I have painted a scene such as you might see anywhere.

Eight Ols are present. You must try to identify them, using these clues: Ols travel in pairs, which do not always look alike. They cannot eat or drink. They are cold to touch, and if they are in human form they try to disguise this by covering themselves with garments, even on the hottest day. Every Ol has the black mark of the Shadow Lord at its core, and whatever shape it takes, this mark appears somewhere on its body. If the mark cannot be hidden by clothing, it is often disguised among many other marks. An Ol can hold a shape without break

for three days. After that, its control falters. The shape wavers for a few seconds before the Ol regains control. This faltering is called the Tremor. It is brief, but unmistakable.

If you suspect you are in the company of an Ol, slip away quietly. Do not try to stand and fight. Ols have enormous strength, and the dread chill of their touch is crippling. They can only be destroyed by being pierced through the heart, which is on the right side instead of the left. Once I saw this happen, but that is another story. I had intended to end this writing here, but I cannot. I learned too late that when Sha-Ban told me of Ols, she was speaking the truth. So I must add something else that she said, for this also might be fact, rather than fancy. She had heard a rumor of a new kind of Ol. Called Grade 2 Ols by those who believe in them, they are said to be far more cunning and difficult to recognize. They can successfully pretend to eat and drink, make their skin seem warm, and go about singly. If this is true, it is disastrous, and shows that the Shadow Lord has continued striving to improve his evil creations. What, then, is to stop him from going further? What if he at last creates a Grade 3 Ol? One that can be so like a human, for example, that it is impossible to distinguish it from the real thing? Or one that can imitate non-living things, as well as living? Then none of us will be safe. I can only pray that it will never come to pass.

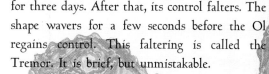

The Glus

This ghastly beast is called the Glus. Its lair is the Maze of the Beast, a series of caverns beneath the sea floor on the west coast, near to where the River Tor joins the sea.

No one who has faced the Glus has lived to tell the tale. But it was my good fortune to meet one who saw it from a distance and survived. For a time after I left the inn I lived in one of the city's drain-tunnels. Other homeless people had taken shelter there. One of these was Ranesh, a rascally young thief. On my first night I heard him crying out in his sleep, moaning of "the Beast" and "the Glus." In the morning, in return for a crust of bread and a wizened apple, he told me his story.

An orphan from a village called Where Waters Meet, he worked on a boat that carried passengers along the River Tor.

The boat was captured by pirates, which are a growing menance on the Tor, it seems. The pirates robbed and killed the passengers, but took Ranesh and his captain to a cave on the coast. There the captain was thrown into a hole that led down to the Maze of the Beast. As his screams of terror drifted upward, the pirates laughed. Then Ranesh was also thrown into the hole — at the end of a rope tied around his waist. The pirates wanted him to work for them, for he was lively and strong. They were showing him what he would suffer if he gave trouble.

Ranesh told me what he saw as he dangled, helpless, in the Beast's lair. It was the picture that still haunted his dreams.

Great spears of stone hung, dripping, from the cavern roof. Everything shone blue and white. The captain lay struggling, his legs wound about with white threads that gripped him hard as stone. A monstrous, white, slug-like creature loomed over him. The stripes on its back were glowing as another mass of white threads sprayed from its gaping red mouth. The captain was covered. The struggles ceased. The Glus settled over him . . . and then Ranesh was pulled to the surface again, and saw no more.

A year after that, he escaped from the pirates during a battle with a rival crew,

and travelled east. He knew he would face the Glus should he ever be re-captured. He far preferred roaming the streets of Del to taking that risk.

I understand his feelings.

The Maze of the Beast has been known since ancient days. It is part of Toran folklore, and is referred to in **The Deltora Annals** several times. But nothing has been written concerning the Glus's origin. I believe the answer lies in a Toran folk song called "Little Enna." The song is at least a hundred years older than the first Maze of the Beast tale. Compared to other Toran songs, it has no great beauty.

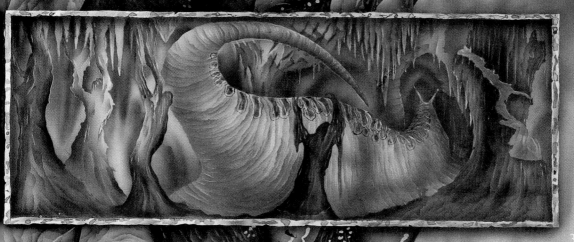

It appears in **The Deltora Annals** in small print, with other songs interesting only to students of ancient Toran culture.

The song tells of a child called Little Enna who, playing by the sea, finds a round, blue stone washed up on the rocks. She loves the stone, and resolves to keep it. As she holds it in her hand it splits in two, and a "sweet sea-worm" crawls out.

Naturally enough, Little Enna's mother is horrified, and tells her daughter to throw the worm back into the sea where it belongs. But Enna [who sounds a silly child indeed!] runs away across the rocks, clutching the "sweet sea-worm" to her heart and crying that if it belongs in the sea, she does also.

At this point a great wave bursts through the rock, catches Little Enna, and pulls her and the "sea-worm" down into the depths. Most scholars have taken this song to be simply a warning to disobedient children. But I think that, like much folklore, it contains a grain of truth.

According to the **Annals**, there is a blowhole among the rocks on a headland near where the River Tor meets the sea. Water gushing from a blowhole might easily be described as a "wave" bursting through rock. And the "sweet sea-worm" dragged down under the rock with Enna could well have been, in young and tiny form, the creature which was to become known, centuries later, as The Glus. This would also explain the final verse of "Little Enna":

Since that sad day, long years have flown,
But still, beneath that seething foam
Where Enna sleeps,
The sea-worm creeps,
And spins its webs of bone-white stone.

Vraal are vicious, fighting beasts, bred in the Shadowlands. They are mentioned once in the last volume of **The Deltora Annals**. At that time, a Vraal had been seen in the foothills of Dread Mountain with a pod of Grey Guards [see Grey Guards, p. 16].

The Guards had the beast on a chain attached to a metal ring fixed to its neck. It was snarling and clawing at them. It was about the size of a man, and every part of it, from slashing claws to lashing tail, was made for destruction.

According to Ranesh, Sha-Ban, and others who have heard Grey Guards talking, Vraal live only to fight and destroy, and are highly intelligent in the ways of battle, though in nothing else. They were bred in captivity, and though a few have escaped to roam wild in the Shadowlands, most are kept in cages beneath a place called the Shadow Arena. They are used, in the words of Guards, for "sport." Prisoners are forced to fight them in the arena, for the entertainment of the crowd.

It is hard to imagine the mind behind such "sport." Or to imagine one that would breed a creature solely so that people will suffer and die. More than anything else, the Vraal symbolizes evil to me. Not the evil of the beast itself, but the evil of the mind that created it.

Vraal

The Guardian

The boy Ranesh watched carefully as I wrote down his words about the Glus. Then he offered to tell me of another monster — a wizard called the Guardian. I feared he was preparing a lie, to earn more food. But when I said that I had nothing to give in return for another tale, he surprised me. He asked me to teach him to read and write. I must have looked surprised, for he blushed angrily, muttering that no doubt I thought he was too stupid to learn. I quickly denied this. I said I would teach him whether or not he told me of the Guardian. But he told me anyway. And as he spoke, his eyes dark with memory, I knew he was telling the truth.

On his way to Del, he had stumbled into the Valley of the Lost — a dismal place, filled with evil, creeping mists. There he met the Guardian — a powerful magician, who can control others with his mind. Everywhere he goes he takes with him four hideous beasts that he calls his "pets." Their names are Hate, Greed, Pride, and Envy. They fawn on their master, but are snarling and savage to strangers.

The Guardian showed Ranesh a magnificent glass palace, filled with riches. Then he challenged Ranesh to play a game of skill. If Ranesh won, he would receive a casket of gold. If he lost, he was doomed to stay in the valley forever.

Ranesh refused. He valued freedom more highly than gold. To his surprise, the wizard simply smiled. "No matter," he said. "It would have been pleasant to defeat you, but I do not need your company. I will have many other subjects soon. Or so I have been told by my master."

He would say no more. But Ranesh ran from the valley, his mind full of questions. Who could be the master of such a powerful being as the Guardian? And who were the subjects soon to fill his miserable domain?
He shuddered with fear, just thinking of it.
And so do I.

39

Nevets

I discovered the monstrous secret of Steven the pedlar on the day I was found by the two fruit-sellers who were Ols [see Ols, p. 32]. Ranesh and I were sitting outside our drain-tunnel shelter. I was giving him a reading lesson, and was delighted by his progress. We did not hear the fruit-sellers approaching until they were right beside us. So old and harmless did they look that, even knowing what I knew, I could hardly believe they were dangerous. Then Steven loomed up behind them. Plainly he had been following them. He had a long spike in his hand. The fruit-sellers spun around, their bodies dissolving and re-forming till they looked like roaring white flames. Hissing, they lunged at Steven. He staggered, the spike falling to the ground. Then, to my terror, bright yellow light began pouring from his body like smoke. Ranesh and I cried out. For another figure was taking shape in the light − a golden giant, savage and terrible, the opposite of Steven in every way. Roaring, the giant snatched up the spike and with two vicious thrusts pierced both Ols through the heart. They fell together in a writhing, melting mass of white.

Then the giant turned on us, growling like a beast. "Run!" Steven roared. We ran deep into the drain-tunnel and huddled there till we heard him calling us. Then we crept out, to find him sitting alone on the grass. "Please forgive my brother," he said calmly. "Nevets is an excellent protector, but sadly he does not always know where to stop." He said no more, but began discussing a safer place where Ranesh and I might stay. Even later, I did not dare to question him. I did not want to anger him. I had no wish to see Nevets again.

Grippers

Grippers are flesh-eating plants that breed quickly and soon cover any area in which they take hold. From a distance they look like any other weed, but when stepped or leaned upon, their leaves part to reveal a fang-lined central "throat" that traps animal and human limbs. When a foot or hand has plunged into a Gripper's "throat," it is injected with a fluid that causes blood to flow freely. The running blood excites the Gripper even further, making it bite and tear the flesh.

Such is the agony and blood loss caused by Gripper bites that few people survive attacks. Victims who are alone collapse and are gradually dragged into the plant's throat, to be digested far beneath the ground. Those who are pulled to safety by companions often die of shock, infection, and loss of blood. These noxious plants are not found in Deltora's north, for they cannot tolerate frost. In the south, however, Grippers have claimed many lives.

To the Jalis tribe, whose territory covers much of the area where Grippers may be found, the danger is a part of life. An ointment made of Gripper flowers, lemon, garlic, sage, and the spittle of a certain frog is used by the Jalis with great effect to treat wounds. Jalis children are warned against Grippers from their earliest days. Nevertheless, **The Deltora Annals** report many tales of young people lost to Grippers through carelessness or foolish, daredevil games.

There was a time when Grippers were kept severely under control. They were weeded out, while still young and tender, by workers wearing thick leather gloves that could resist attacks. Just before the **Annals** ceased to be kept, however, Queen Elspeth's chief advisor announced that the Gripper weeding program was to end. He said it was unnecessary and too expensive.

Since that time, I hear, Grippers have multiplied enormously, making vast areas of good farming land useless. Farmers have attempted to fight the menace on their own, without success. Most have been forced to place stepping-stones through affected fields, so that at least they can cross the areas in safety.

It is one of the greatest complaints the people of the south have against the palace, but King Alton is ignorant of it. He was told by Prandine that Grippers became extinct long ago, and he believes it. As did I until I escaped from the palace and discovered how life truly was in Deltora.

Blood Lily Island, the smaller of two islands lying off Deltora's southwest tip, is completely covered by the flowers for which it is named. I group Blood Lilies with Grippers because, though Blood Lilies have no means of attacking humans by themselves, they are one side of a deadly partnership.

Small, flesh-eating beasts called Fleshbanes live closely with the Blood Lilies, and use them to trap their prey. As you can see from the painting overleaf, Fleshbanes at rest look very like Blood Lily flowers. Perfectly disguised, they cling to the Lily stems, waiting. Birds and animals are attracted to the Blood Lilies' color and scent. Humans, too, when ignorant of the plants' dangers, find the urge to walk among them almost irresistible. But the sticky pollen that coats Blood Lily stamens sinks easily through fur, feathers, and clothing and has an immediate, numbing effect on the skin. A single smear is enough to reduce feeling in a large area.

Fleshbanes then silently emerge from cover and attach themselves to the numbed place. They cut through any covering with their razor-sharp pincers, and begin to attack the flesh beneath, without the victim being aware of it. So powerful is the pollen's effect that a person's back and legs can be covered by dozens, even hundreds, of Fleshbanes before he or she

Blood Lilies
and Fleshbanes

notices. By this time so much damage has been done, and blood loss is so devastating, that death almost always results.

The Fleshbanes repay the Blood Lilies by keeping them free of pests and by burying the carcasses of victims around their roots, to provide them with a constant source of food.

Naturally, there have been efforts made to use Blood Lily nectar for pain relief. The *Annals* record experiments made by Jalis knights of old, who visited the island clad in full armor. They found that pollen from a picked Blood Lily

loses its ability to numb flesh after only two hours. This, strangely enough, is the exact time it takes to return to the mainland from Blood Lily Island. And sadly, all attempts to grow Blood Lilies away from the island have failed. Without the protection of the Fleshbanes, and away from their natural soil, these strange plants soon wither and die. They have no use for human partnership, it seems. Keep well clear of their island, unless you wish to join the thousands of others whose bones enrich its soil.

Dragons

It is generally believed that the Deltoran Dragons are extinct, having been at last wiped out by the Shadow Lord's Seven Ak-Baba [see The Seven Ak-Baba, p. 18]. Many farmers, whose herds were preyed upon by Dragons, say this is no loss. Those who know old tales of girls being carried off so their long hair could line Dragons' nests, agree. More thoughtful students of life think otherwise.

In general, Dragons hunted only to satisfy their hunger and feed their young. As soon as villagers began to leave out tresses of hair in Spring, for example, Dragons no longer took maidens at nesting time. Dragons were dangerous, there is no doubt. But they had no particular wish to harm. Native to Deltora, they were part of the natural order and owed no loyalty to any creature other than themselves. The Seven Ak-Baba, which can now patrol Deltoran skies without hindrance, are a very different matter.

Furthermore, I suspect that Dragons, the most ancient of Deltora's beasts, were linked with the land more closely than we understand. The Dragons were divided into seven breeds — just as the original Deltoran people were divided into seven tribes. Each breed shared its territory with one tribe, and, most interestingly, each had its own color.

The undersides of all were the same, changing color with the sky so that flying beasts would be hard to see from the ground. Each breed, however, shone a different color on the back — the color of its territory's totem stone, the gem which became, in the time of Adin, part of the magic Belt of Deltora.

Thus, the Del Dragons were golden, like the topaz.

Those of Raladin were ruby red. The Dragons of the Plains shone with all the colors of the rainbow, like the opal.

The Mere Dragons were darkest blue with points of silver, like the lapis lazuli.

The Dragons of Dread Mountain were emerald green. The Toran Dragons were purple, like the amethyst. And the scales of the Dragons of Jalis glittered like the diamond.

This is a great mystery, and one which must make us all think carefully before rejoicing at the Dragons' disappearance. If they have truly gone from our land, we could have lost far more than we realize.

But I am not convinced they have gone. My reading over the years has given me great respect for the wisdom of these beasts. It would not surprise me if, after centuries of loss, the last Dragons decided to hide themselves so that their race could continue. I hope with all my heart that it is so. The decline of the Dragons is a powerful symbol of the way in which, slowly but surely, the balance of Deltora's natural world has been twisted and ravaged by the evil mind that broods over the Shadowlands.

And the corruption of the natural world is itself a symbol of what has happened to our society. Once united, thriving, and strong, the people are divided, suffering, and fearful. The heirs of Adin, once our trusted leaders, guardians of the magic Belt of Deltora, are locked away from us, and kept in ignorance of our fate.

I heard this morning that King Alton is gravely ill. If he dies, young Prince Endon will take his place. There is neither grief nor rejoicing in Del. The people no longer care what goes on in the palace.

Ranesh says hunger and misery rule, and it does not matter who is king. Dark clouds have been gathering over Deltora for a long, long time.

I fear a great storm is coming.

And it is very near.